Greedy Guts
and Belly Busters

Retold by Rose Impey

Illustrated by *Anthony Lewis*

ORCHARD BOOKS

Other titles in this series:

I Spy, Pancakes and Pies

Bad Boys and Naughty Girls

If Wishes were Fishes

Silly Sons and Dozy Daughters

Ugly Dogs and Slimy Frogs

ORCHARD BOOKS
96 Leonard Street, London EC2A 4XD
Orchard Books Australia
14 Mars Road, Lane Cove, NSW 2066
First published in Great Britain in 1999
First paperback publication 2000
Text © Rose Impey 1999
Illustrations © Anthony Lewis 1999
The rights of Rose Impey to be identified as the author
and Anthony Lewis as the illustrator of this work
have been asserted by them in accordance with the
Copyright, Designs and Patents Act, 1988.
A CIP catalogue record for this book is available
from the British Library.
1 86039 959 2 (hardback)
1 86039 960 6 (paperback)
1 3 5 7 9 10 8 6 4 2 (hardback)
3 5 7 9 10 8 6 4 (paperback)
Printed in Great Britain

★ CONTENTS ★

★ Fat cat Munchalot ★

There was once a cat with a
colossal appetite. Eat! Goodness,
how that cat could eat.

He grew fatter and fatter, while the old couple who owned him grew poorer and poorer. In the end they decided the cat just had to go, before he ate them out of house and home.

So one morning the old woman poured a saucer of cream. "Here puss, puss, puss," she called. "This is your last meal in this house."

Well, Fat Cat Munchalot wasn't happy about that. So what did he do? First he ate the cream and then he ate the jug.

And then he ate the old woman
too. In one GULP!

Then off he went to see what
else he could find.

He found the old man in the
garden digging up parsnips. The
old man was surprised to see the
cat looking fatter than ever.

"Pussy cat, pussy cat, how did
you get so fat?" said the old man.

Said Munchalot,
"*I ate the cream*
and *the jug*
and the old woman, too.

And now, old man, I think I'm
going to eat...you!"

And he did. He ate the old man – gulp! – *and* his barrowful of parsnips.

Then off he went to see what else he could find.

He found the dairymaid, sitting on a stool, milking the cow.

"Oh, pussy cat, pussy cat, how did you get so fat?" said the dairymaid.

Said Munchalot,
"I ate the cream
and the jug
and the old woman too.
And the old man
and his barrowful of parsnips.

And now…I think I'm going
to eat you!"

And he swallowed the dairymaid,
just like that. *And* her stool. *And*
the cow; horns, hooves and all.

But, that cat *still* wasn't full. So
off he went to see what else he
could find.

He found the farmer driving his cart up the lane. The farmer stopped and stared at Munchalot, who was the fattest cat he had ever seen.

"Oh, pussy cat, pussy cat, how did you get so fat?" said the farmer.

Said Munchalot,
"I ate the cream
and *the jug*
and *the old woman too.*
And the old man
and his barrowful of parsnips,
and the dairymaid and the cow.

And now…I think I'm going
to eat you!"

That fat cat opened his mouth and swallowed the farmer – gulp! – and his cart full of hay.

But he *still* wasn't full. So off he went along the lane until he met a shepherd with his flock of sheep.

The shepherd couldn't get past Munchalot, who was nearly filling the lane.

"Oh, pussy cat, pussy cat, how did you get so fat?" said the shepherd.

Said Munchalot,
"I ate the cream
and the jug
and the old woman too.
And the old man
and his barrowful of parsnips,
and the dairymaid
and the cow,
and the farmer
and his cart.

And now...I think I'm going
to eat you!"

Which he did. Yes, *and* all the
sheep, every last one of them. And
still that cat wasn't full. So, off he
went to see what else he could find.

He waddled and he rolled into
the village and up to the church
where there was a wedding.

The bride squealed with laughter.
"Oh, pussy cat, pussy cat, how
did you get so fat?"
But the bride didn't laugh for
long.

Said Munchalot,
"I ate the cream
and the jug
and the old woman too.
And the old man
and his barrowful of parsnips,
and the dairymaid
and the cow,
and the farmer
and his cart,
and the shepherd
and his flock.

And now...I think I'm going
to eat you."

Then he ate the bride – gulp! –
and the groom – gulp! – and all
the wedding guests, in their best
clothes, one after another. What
a day!

I suppose I don't need to tell you
what he did next. That's right, he
waddled off to see what else he
could find.

Slowly, ever so slowly, Fat Cat Munchalot went waddle, waddle, roll, roll, through the village. At the end of the village he came to a bridge. And on that bridge stood Old Billy-Goat with his two big horns.

"Oh, pussy cat, pussy cat, how did you get so fat?" said Old Billy-Goat.

Fat Cat Munchalot grinned and
licked his lips, and said,

"*I ate the cream*
and the jug
and the old woman too,
and the old man
and his barrowful of parsnips,
and the dairymaid
and the cow,
and the farmer and his cart,
and the shepherd
and his flock,
and the wedding with the bride.

And now…I think I'm going
to eat you."

But Old Billy-Goat shook his
head. "You'll have to fight me
first," he said. He lowered his
head and butted Fat Cat
Munchalot right off that bridge.

Up, up he sailed like a big
balloon and then he dropped,
down, down, down into the river.
When he hit the water he burst
with a tremendous POP!

Out came the
bride and the
wedding party;

the shepherd
and his flock
of sheep;

the farmer and
his cart;

the dairymaid
and the cow;

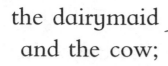

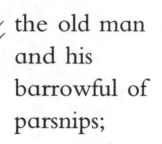

the old man
and his
barrowful of
parsnips;

and the old
woman too.

And her
cream jug
with the cream
still in it.

Out they came and off they ran, all as good as new.

But I'm afraid I can't say the same for Fat Cat Munchalot, who was never quite right again.

He ate and he ate:
He just wouldn't stop,
Till he met old Billy-Goat
And then he went POP!

POP!

An Eating Match with a Troll

Trolls are trouble. Take my advice, never trust one. This is the story of a troll that came to a bad end.

Once upon a time there was a poor farmer who was getting old and ever deeper in debt. All he had left was a bit of forest and three sons who didn't know the meaning of the word 'work'.

One day the farmer told his lazy sons they must stir themselves. They must go out and cut down the forest and sell the wood, before they all starved.

So the next day off went the eldest son with an axe over his shoulder. He'd just started to chop the first tree when up comes a big, bossy troll.

"What are you doing, chopping in my forest?" roared the troll. "Now I shall have to kill you and eat you."

Well, the eldest son didn't fancy that. He threw down his axe and ran off home as if his feet were on fire.

When he told his father what
had happened, his father roared
too. "You chicken-heart. You
weak-willed worm! Why, when
I was young, I wouldn't have let
a troll tell *me* what to do."

The next day, the second son
went off with an axe over his
shoulder.

He did no better than the first. He'd just started chopping when up comes the big, bossy troll and says, "What are you doing, chopping in my forest? Now I shall have to kill you and eat you."

But the
second son
didn't wait
around to be
eaten, either.
He raced
home and his
father roared
at him:
"You lily-liver!
You mouse!
You jellyfish!
Why, when
I was young,
I wouldn't
have let a
troll tell *me*
what to do."

On the third day the youngest son, who they called the Ash Lad, decided to try his luck.

"You?" sneered his brothers. "What can you do? You're hardly out of nappies!"

But the Ash Lad said nothing.

He found
himself an
axe and asked
his mother for
one of her
curd cheeses
for his lunch.
They were
delicious —
round, smooth
as a stone
and white
as milk. The
Ash Lad put
one in his
leather rucksack
and went off
to the forest.

He'd only been chopping a few minutes, when up came the big, bossy troll.

"What are you doing, chopping in my forest?" he roared.

"My father's forest," the Ash Lad corrected him.

"We'll soon see about that," roared the troll. "But first I'm going to kill you and eat you."

"Oh, hold your tongue," said the boy.

The troll went red with rage. He wasn't used to being talked to like that! But do you think the Ash Lad took any notice? Not at all. He bent down and picked up a flat white stone.

"You see this?" he said, holding it out to the troll in one hand. At the same time he reached into his rucksack with the other and pulled out his mother's curd cheese.

"If you don't hold your noise,
I'll squeeze you like these stones,
until the water runs out of you."
And he squeezed his mother's
cheese until the water ran down
his arm in a stream.

The troll didn't like the look of that, I can tell you. He soon changed his tune. "Perhaps dear lad, you'd let me help you with your chopping?"

"I might let you," said the lad. "If you think you can keep up with me."

The troll worked all day until the sweat poured off him. He chopped as if his life depended on it. By evening half the forest was felled.

Then the troll invited the Ash Lad back to his house for supper. The lad went along with him; he wasn't afraid. He had other tricks up his sleeve yet.

When they came to his house, the troll started to lay the fire. He told the lad to fetch water from the well to make porridge. But the two iron buckets in the corner were so heavy the lad couldn't even lift them.

The Ash Lad kicked one. "Those thimbles!" he said, "I wouldn't waste my time. Show me where the well is and I'll carry it back here for you."

The troll didn't want to lose his well, thank you very much.

"Never mind, dear lad," he said. "You start the fire. I'll fetch the water. "

So the Ash Lad lit the fire and
the troll started to cook a huge
pot of thick, creamy porridge.
Enough to feed an army of trolls.

When the Ash Lad saw how
much there was to eat, he said,
"I've got a good idea. Let's you
and me have an eating match."

The troll was all for that. He
was a greedy beast; and he had a
stomach big enough for the job.

The troll ate and ate and ate.
He was so busy spooning the
porridge into his big greedy
mouth, he hardly looked up.

The Ash Lad ate steadily too.
But he had tucked his leather
rucksack inside his shirt. For every
spoonful he ate, he spooned ten
into his rucksack.

When it was full and ready to overflow, the Ash Lad smacked his lips and said, "This is such good porridge I could eat the same again. In fact I think I will."

The troll was surprised. *He'd* eaten so much he was almost full to bursting.

"I'll just make a bit of room first, though," said the lad. He took out his knife and – snick! snack! snick! – he cut through his rucksack and out poured the porridge.

The troll's eyes were wide with fear. "Didn't that hurt?" he asked.

"Hardly felt a thing," said the lad. "Why don't you try it?"

Can you believe it? The stupid troll did. And that was the end of him.

Snick! Snack! Snick!
What a good trick.
The troll was past mending
So this is the ending.

Fat Cat Munchalot is a well-known story which comes from Scandinavia, and so does *An Eating Match with a Troll*. Similar stories about squeezing water out of a stone can be found in a number of other European countries too.

Here are some more stories you might like to read:

About Big Appetites:

Otesahnek the Wooden Doll
from *The Barefoot Book of
        Strange and Spooky Stories*
by Andrew Fusek Peters
(Barefoot Books)

Unanana and the Enormous One-Tusked Elephant
from *The Orchard Book of Magical Tales*
by Margaret Mayo
(Orchard Books)

About Other Tricksters:

Two Giants
from *Tales for the Telling*
by Edna O'Brien
(Pavilion Books)

The Pot of Gold
from *The Orchard Book of
        Irish Fairy Tales and Legends*
by Una Leavy
(Orchard Books)